Prologue
I0745256

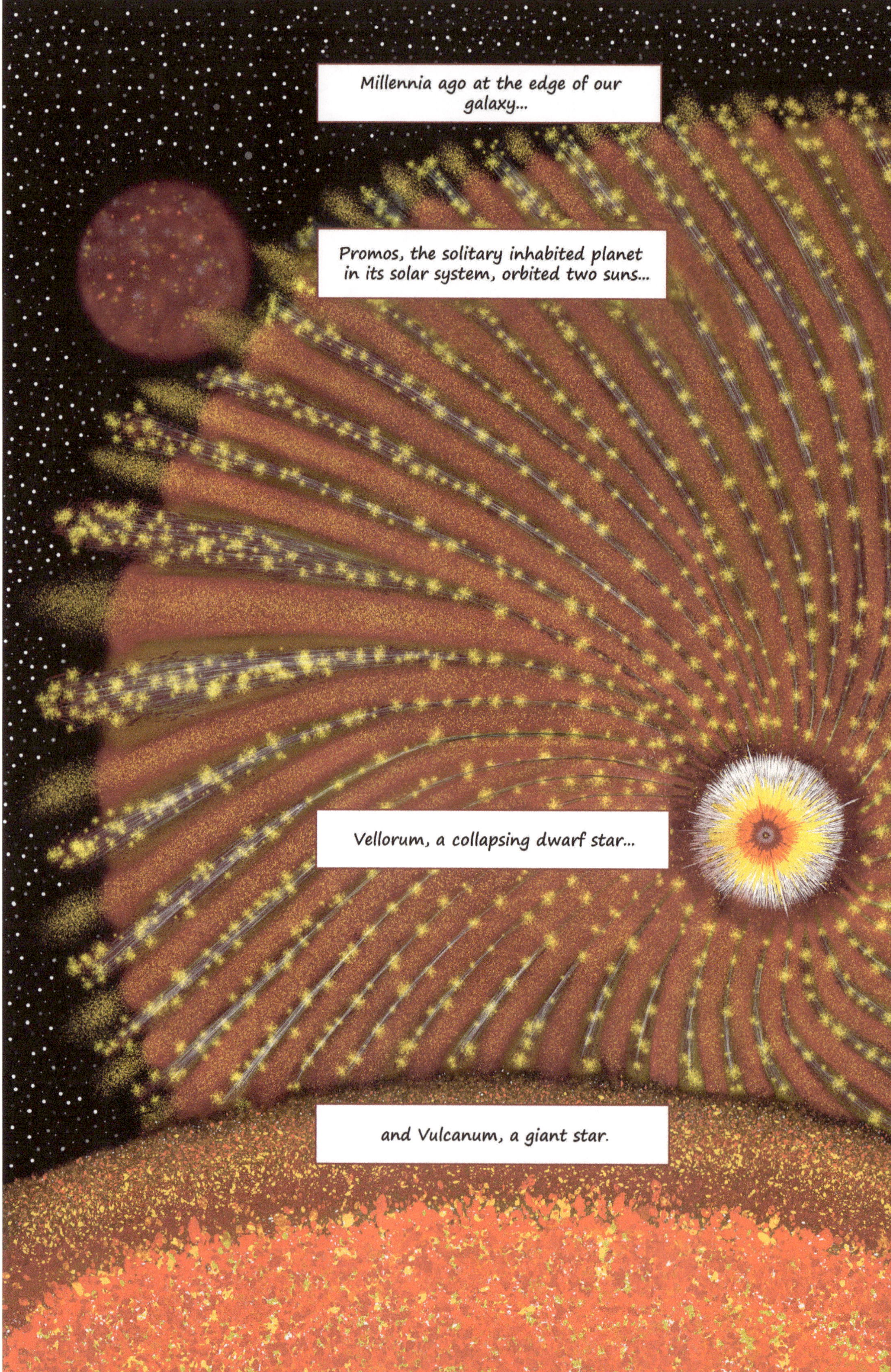

Millennia ago at the edge of our galaxy...
Promos, the solitary inhabited planet in its solar system, orbited two suns...
Vellorum, a collapsing dwarf star...
and Vulcanum, a giant star.

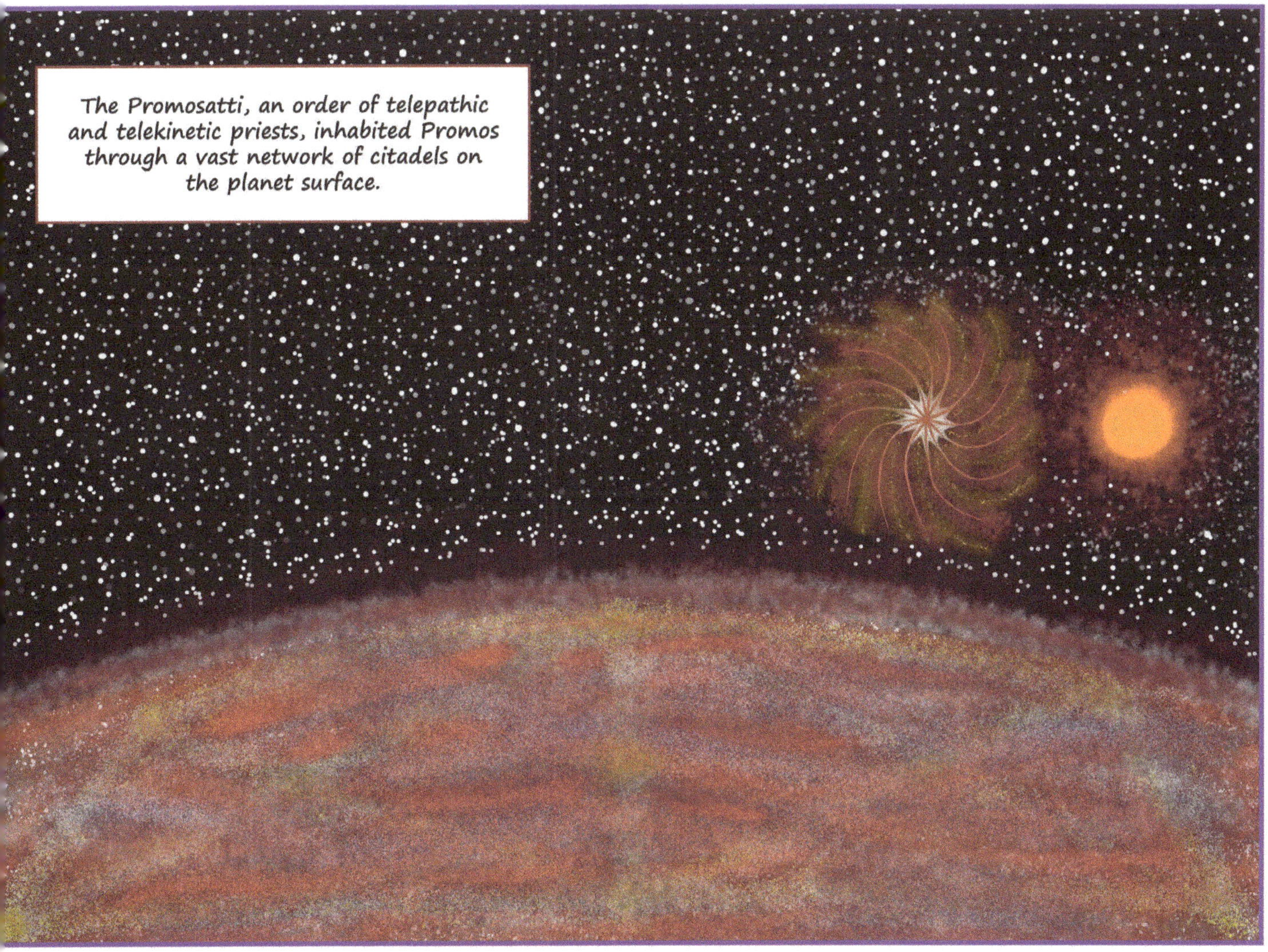

The Promosatti, an order of telepathic and telekinetic priests, inhabited Promos through a vast network of citadels on the planet surface.

Within the Mountains of Fyre, the walls of Promosthenia encircled the Temple of Towers, home of the high priest, Anormayne.

Chapter One

The Gate of Drakaar

Pillars of Dromos

Plane of Despayre

Gate of Drakaar

Beyond the Mountains of Fyre and the Plane of Despayre, the Gate of Drakaar sealed the Underverse from the mortal plane.
The fallen angel and ruler of the Underverse, Falonayus, breached the energy barrier which sealed the gate.

The Gate of Drakaar cannot hold me. I have come to the mortal plane for my revenge against the Promosatti.

I shall fly to the Pillars of Dromos.

Below me, the site of the War of Dromos, the Plane of Despayre, will become my new battleground.
Before me, the Pillars of Dromos stand as a monument to a war the Promosatti think they won.

6

The proud Promosatti built these pillars to glorify themselves, yet I know their secret fortress, the Crypt of Dromos, lies beneath.

Durlyn, you descended into your fortress below, and sealed yourself inside. I will make my own entrance, and unleash my apostle to rule the mortal plane.

Durlyn, deep inside your fortress, feel the heat of my fire, which will consume you and the Promosatti.

Protheus, my thoughts reach you in your prison below. The Divine has sent Shor Tayle to the mortal plane, to minister to our comrades on a distant world. I shall send you to this planet, to conduct a war against Shor Tayle and his followers.

Chapter Two

Journey to the Crypt

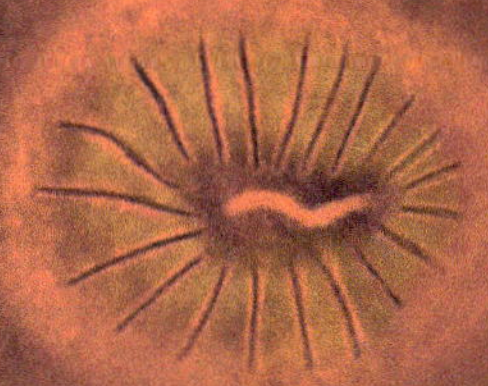

From the spires of Promosthenia, two Promosatti priests gaze down upon the rugged landscape of Promos below.
Anormayne, I felt a tremor deep within Promos this morning.
Urtur, I sense a great crater has formed many leagues from here.

Where is this crater located, master?
In my mind, I see the crater between the Mountains of Fyre, and the Plane of Despayre.

I sense the thoughts of my old master, Durlyn, deep within the crater.
You told me stories of Durlyn ages ago, when I trained as your apprentice.

Durlyn left my side long before I became high priest. He journeyed far into the Mountains of Fyre.
Is this the first time you sensed him since then?

Yes, Urtur. I feel a great evil presence near him. I must find Durlyn, and face the evil now.
Anormayne, I must journey with you. I cannot allow you, our high priest, to face this evil alone.

Urtur, prepare the Promosatti for the pilgrimage to the Temple of the Obelisk. Joffar will travel with me to find Durlyn.
Yes, master. I will go to the temple, start the morning prayers, and prepare the Promosatti for travel.

Before I travel, I shall go to my chambers in the Temple of Towers for my journey staff, Joffar.

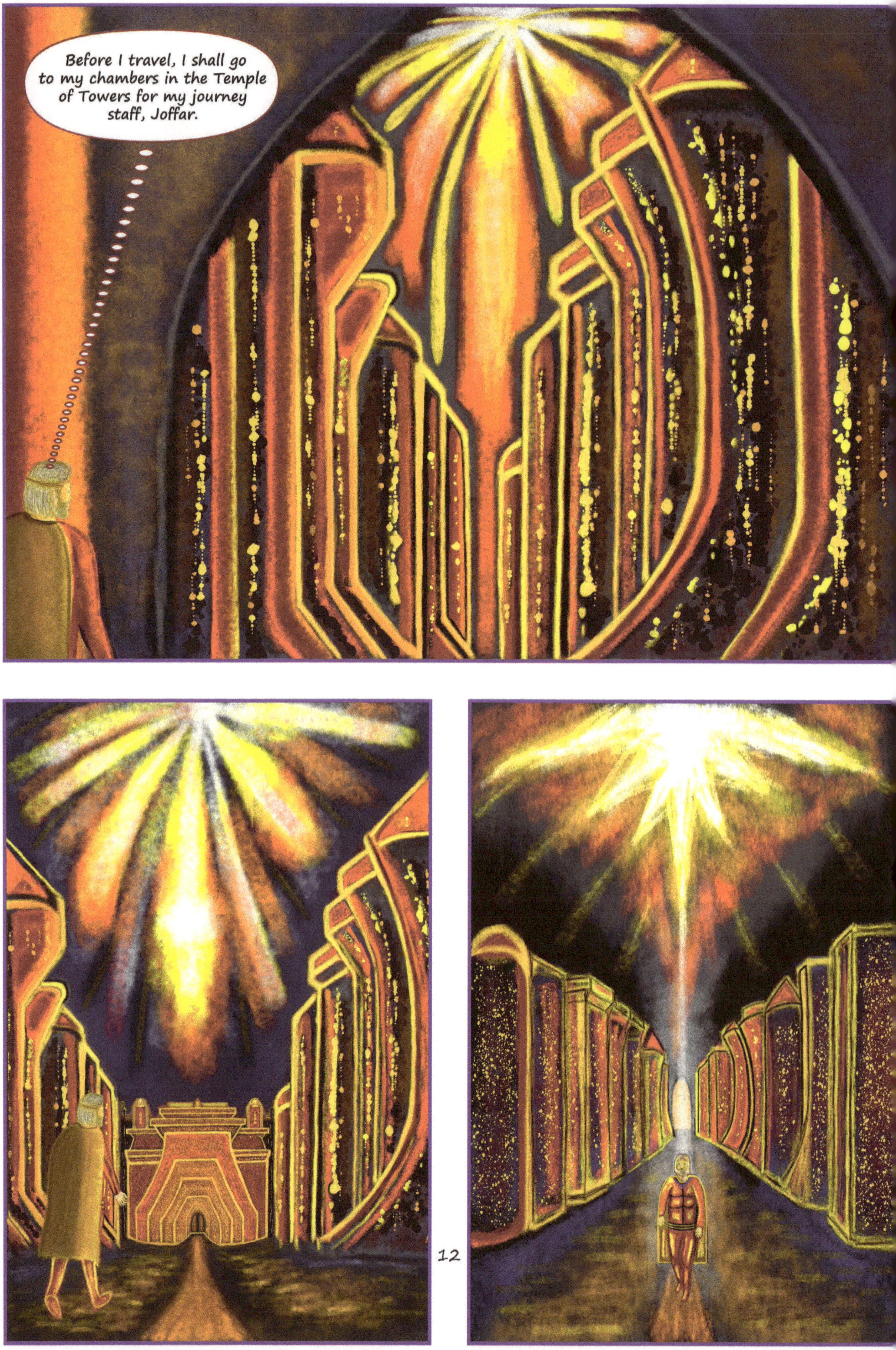

12

The Temple of Towers...

While Urtur finishes morning prayers, I shall go to my chambers down the hall.

Let us lift up our prayers to the Divine, as we prepare for our pilgrimage to the Temple of the Obelisk.
Almost there...

My chambers...

Joffar, my friend, we travel together to see our old master, Durlyn.

I remember when we first met, Joffar.
I visited you with Durlyn when I was a young apprentice.
I am here as you requested, Durlyn.
Thank you, Anormayne.
Durlyn, I am dying. Anormayne must take my place by your side.
Joffar, we must seek guidance from our guardian angel, Gabriolus.

Gabriolus, you have arrived.
Perform the spiritual transfer ritual. Use this staff to hold the spirit of Joffar.
Joffar, do you consent to the spiritual transfer ritual?
Yes, my high priest, I will serve you again within this staff. Afterward, I will travel with Gabriolus to eternal paradise, the Oververse.
17

Sar Sayle!

Durlyn,
I live inside
this staff!

Anormayne, I remain inside this staff, ready to serve you.

Yes, Urtur. I just had a memory of my first meeting with Joffar.

I shall leave now with Joffar to find Durlyn. I shall meet you at the Temple of the Obelisk as soon as possible.

Anormayne, are you alright?

Please summon me if you require my assistance. Farewell.

The city gates...

By leaving Promosthenia early, I have escaped public notice of my departure.

The Mountains of Fyre...

21

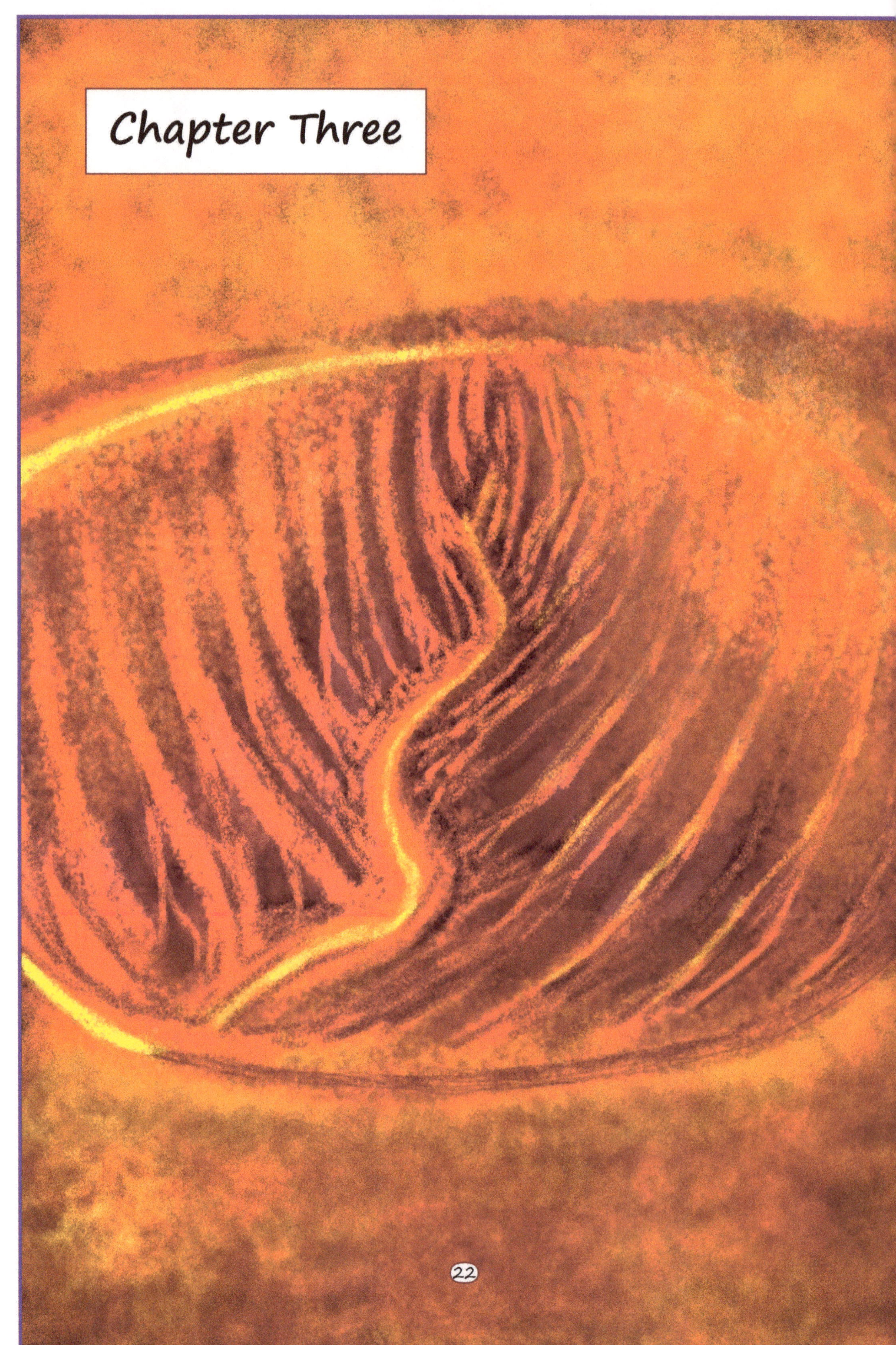
Chapter Three

The Crypt of Dromos

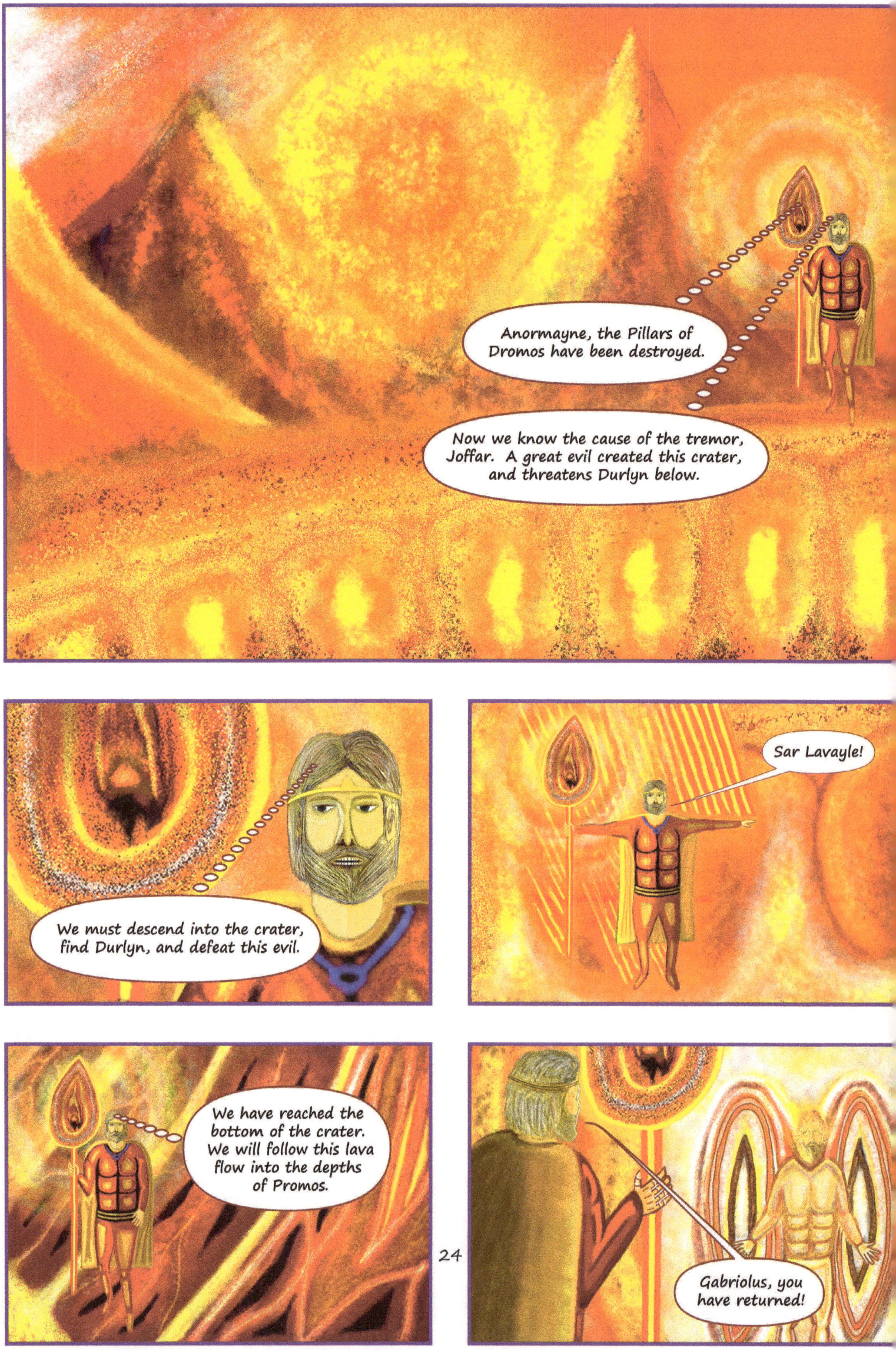

Anormayne, the Pillars of Dromos have been destroyed.
Now we know the cause of the tremor, Joffar. A great evil created this crater, and threatens Durlyn below.
We must descend into the crater, find Durlyn, and defeat this evil.

Sar Lavayle!

We have reached the bottom of the crater. We will follow this lava flow into the depths of Promos.

Gabriolus, you have returned!

24

Have you seen Durlyn?
I have seen him often since he has been here. I shall take you to him.
First, I must tell you of our desperate situation.

The Divine has sent His messenger, Shor Tayle, to a distant world, Urth, to deliver His words of love.
Falonayus has entered this crater to release Protheus from prison.
Durlyn concealed this prison from me. He told me stories of Protheus, our high priest, who was corrupted by Falonayus.
He commanded a Dromosatti army against us in the War of Dromos.

How did Protheus arrive here?
In the final battle, your parents, Falron and Dryelle, fused into your staff.
Using their combined energies, Durlyn defeated Protheus, and placed him beneath us.

After the war, Durlyn became high priest, and secretly built this crypt. Ellenos became high priestess after Durlyn's reign. She assumed Durlyn's role as your new mentor.
Durlyn returned to this crypt, to become the Keeper of Dromos, and prevent Protheus from escaping.
Has Shor Tayle shifted the balance of power, prompting Falonayus to release Protheus, and start a new war against the Promosatti?

His plan is more devious. Falonayus intends to send Protheus through a portal from Promos to Urth, to conquer this world, and destroy Shor Tayle.
Falonayus plans to create a new Dromosatti army on Promos.
Gabriolus, lead the way. We must find Durlyn to join us against Falonayus.

Tell me more about this portal.
I built the portal on the Mount of the Heavens, as directed by the Divine, to take our disobedient people to Urth for exile millennia ago.
The Promosatti remained on Promos to teach our faithful ones. I have shared this knowledge only with our high priests, who have kept this secret for ages.

Behold the crypt entrance, sealed by Durlyn long ago.
Falonayus exposed this by destroying the Pillars of Dromos, creating this crater.
Lead on with haste. We must reach Durlyn before Falonayus.

This corridor follows the lava flow to a chamber containing a massive pool of molten rock.
Passages beyond lead to chambers containing Durlyn and Protheus.
If Falonayus has taken the passage leading to Protheus, we may find Durlyn before Falonayus.

The path to
Durlyn seems clear.

The light leads us
to the left path.

Gabriolus, why have I
been unable to feel the
presence of Durlyn until
this morning?

Durlyn wears the
Helm of Dromos to prevent
his enemies from sensing his
location. He removed the
helm today to summon
you with his thoughts.

At last, we have arrived. Durlyn awaits us beyond a short corridor.
I sense Durlyn beyond. Why am I unable to sense Falonayus?

Falonayus wears the Crown of Drakaar, preventing you from sensing his location.

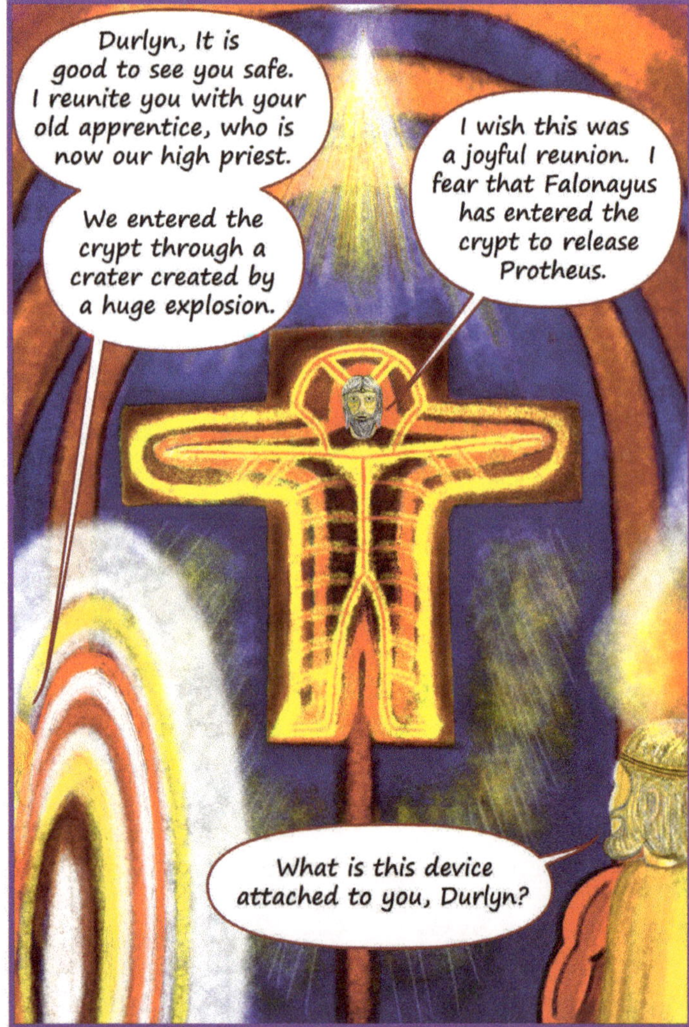

Durlyn, It is good to see you safe. I reunite you with your old apprentice, who is now our high priest.
We entered the crypt through a crater created by a huge explosion.
I wish this was a joyful reunion. I fear that Falonayus has entered the crypt to release Protheus.
What is this device attached to you, Durlyn?

28

It is the Chronomycron of Dromos. Gabriolus created it to keep me alive, so I could guard Protheus, and prevent his escape.

I have an option for you, Durlyn, if you wish it. I carry Shor Brayle, the Soul Bringer of the Heavens.
Anormayne can perform the spiritual transfer ritual, placing your spirit inside Shor Brayle, so you can travel with us to face our enemies.
Durlyn, we need you with us as we face Falonayus and Protheus. Only with your strength added to ours, can we hope to prevail.

I built this crypt to bury Protheus and his Dromosatti army, to hide his darkness from our people.
Falonayus plans to release Protheus and his darkness.
My spirit must go with you to restore balance, or I must surrender all I have fought for through the ages.

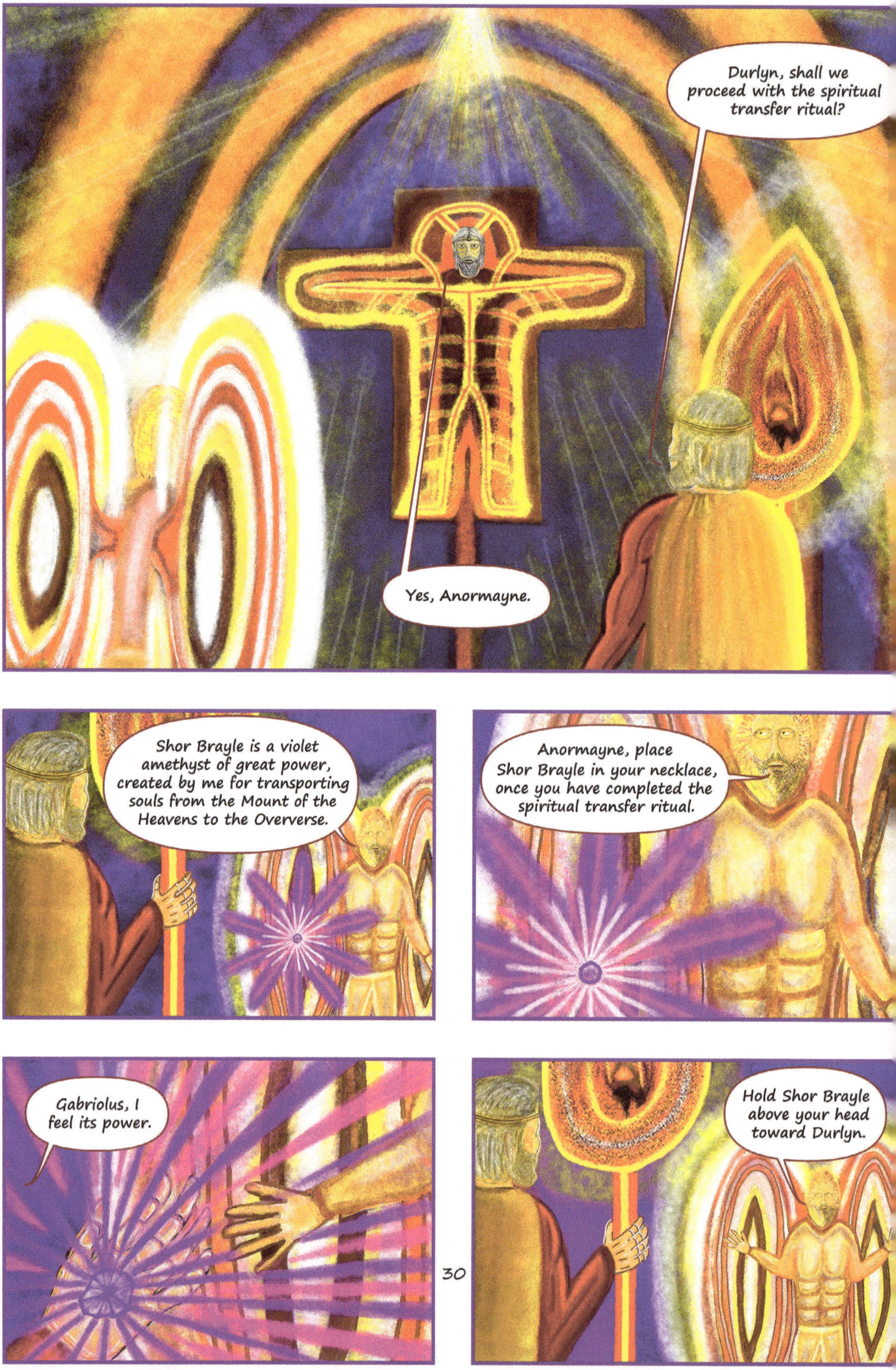

Durlyn, shall we proceed with the spiritual transfer ritual?
Yes, Anormayne.

Shor Brayle is a violet amethyst of great power, created by me for transporting souls from the Mount of the Heavens to the Oververse.

Anormayne, place Shor Brayle in your necklace, once you have completed the spiritual transfer ritual.

Gabriolus, I feel its power.

Hold Shor Brayle above your head toward Durlyn.

Sar Sayle!

Anormayne,
I live within
Shor Brayle!

Durlyn, I shall carry you with me, inside Shor Brayle, seated in my necklace.
I anticipate a battle ahead. You will perform defensive rituals, and Joffar will perform offensive rituals. This should provide a tactical advantage.
Anormayne, I am ready to assist you in any way.

The dark path leads to the dungeon entrance ahead.

Protheus waits ahead inside the dungeon. The spirit of Protheus is imprisoned in a sphere, while his body remains comatose in a sarcophagus below.
Is this true, Durlyn?
Yes, Anormayne. I used the spiritual transfer ritual to place the spirit of Protheus into the sphere.

I see no sign of Falonayus.

The sphere and sarcophagus containing Protheus are intact.

Falonayus!
Welcome Anormayne, Durlyn, Joffar, and Gabriolus. Allow me to show my affection for you!

Durlyn, Sar Shayle!

Durlyn, your spiritual shield is holding!

Joffar, Sar Prayle!

AAAGGGHHH!
Joffar, your spiritual projectile hit Falonayus!

Gabriolus, finish him!
Falonayus, I banish you to the Underverse, with the holy light of the Divine!

It burns me!

You have won this battle, but you have not won the war!

We will meet again!

The roof is collapsing!
Falonayus is taking the sphere containing the spirit of Protheus!

We must pursue Falonayus!

Sar Lavayle!

I see light from outside of the crypt.

37

I sense Urtur has arrived at the Temple of the Obelisk.

Chapter Four

Temple of the Obelisk

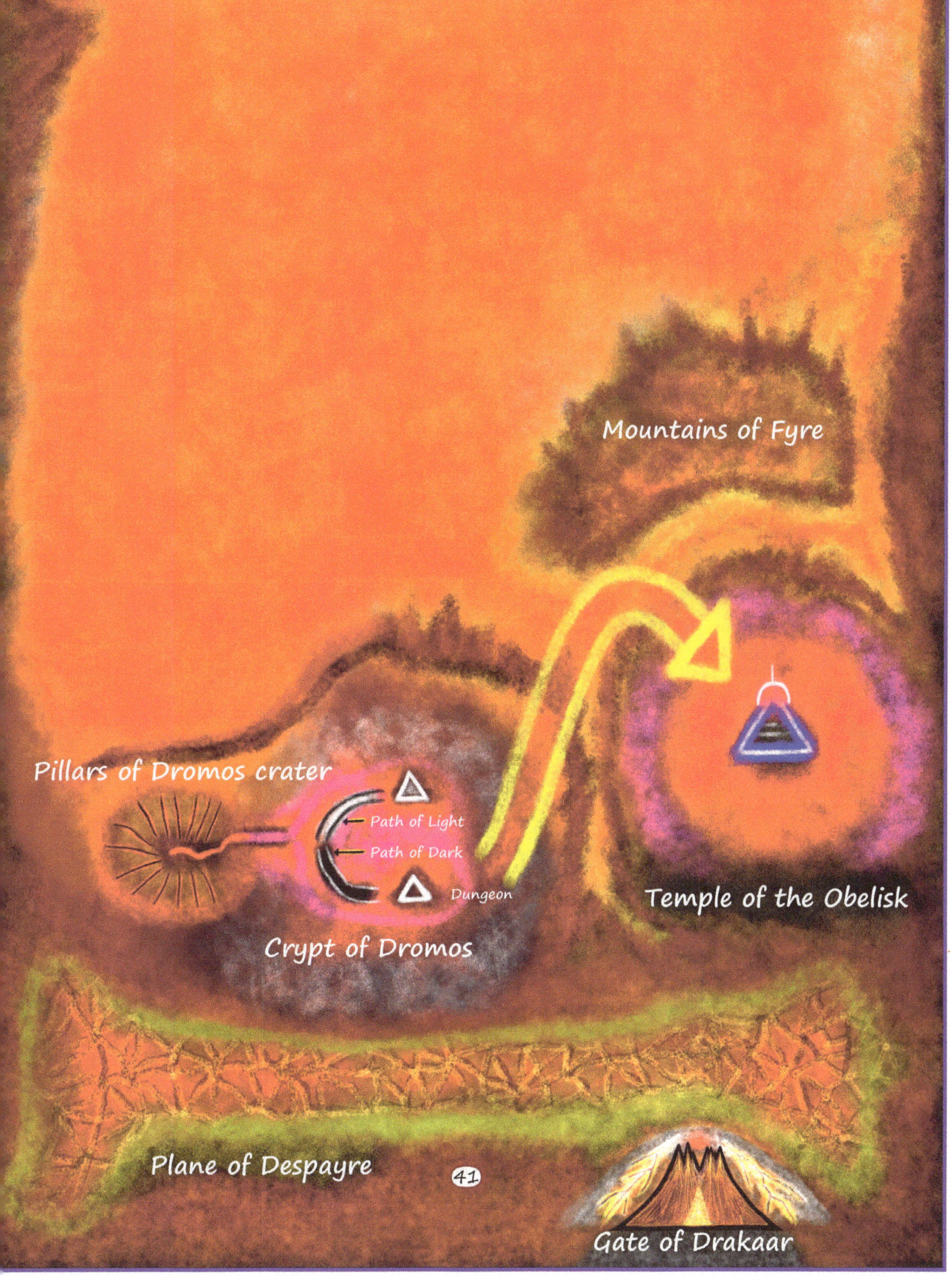

Mountains of Fyre

Pillars of Dromos crater
Path of Light
Path of Dark
Dungeon
Crypt of Dromos

Temple of the Obelisk

Plane of Despayre

Gate of Drakaar

Calayre, I sense that Anormayne is approaching our location.
I sense that his mind is troubled, Urtur.
The Temple of the Obelisk is ahead!

I shall inform Ellenos, the keeper of the temple, that Anormayne is on his way.

I shall inform her of his journey to investigate the crater.

Ellenos, our high priest is on his way.
Urtur, in my mind, I have followed Anormayne through his entire journey.
He pursues Falonayus. We must form a defensive perimeter around the temple entrance.

Sar Shayle!

If your defensive shield fails, Urtur, I will use my Amulet of Shorcuyle to drive Falonayus away from our temple.

Urtur, the roof is exploding!
Ellenos, prepare to use your amulet!

How ironic, Protheus. Your evil soul will possess Urtur, beloved apprentice of Anormayne.
I shall call you Protur, and you will conquer the galaxy in my name.

Falonayus has breached your defensive shield and my protective aura!
He is paralyzing all of us!

I must meditate to overcome my paralysis, and restore my protective aura.
Make haste Ellenos. Falonayus is approaching!

Protheus, I transfer your soul to Urtur!

Ellenos, help me!
Urtur!

I am Protur.
Kneel before
me or die!

Falonayus, in the name of the Divine, I dispel you from this temple with my Amulet of Shorcuyle!

Come, Protur. We must leave. I have another mission for you.

Ellenos, you have driven away Falonayus and Protur!
Divine light, focused through my amulet, has driven them away.

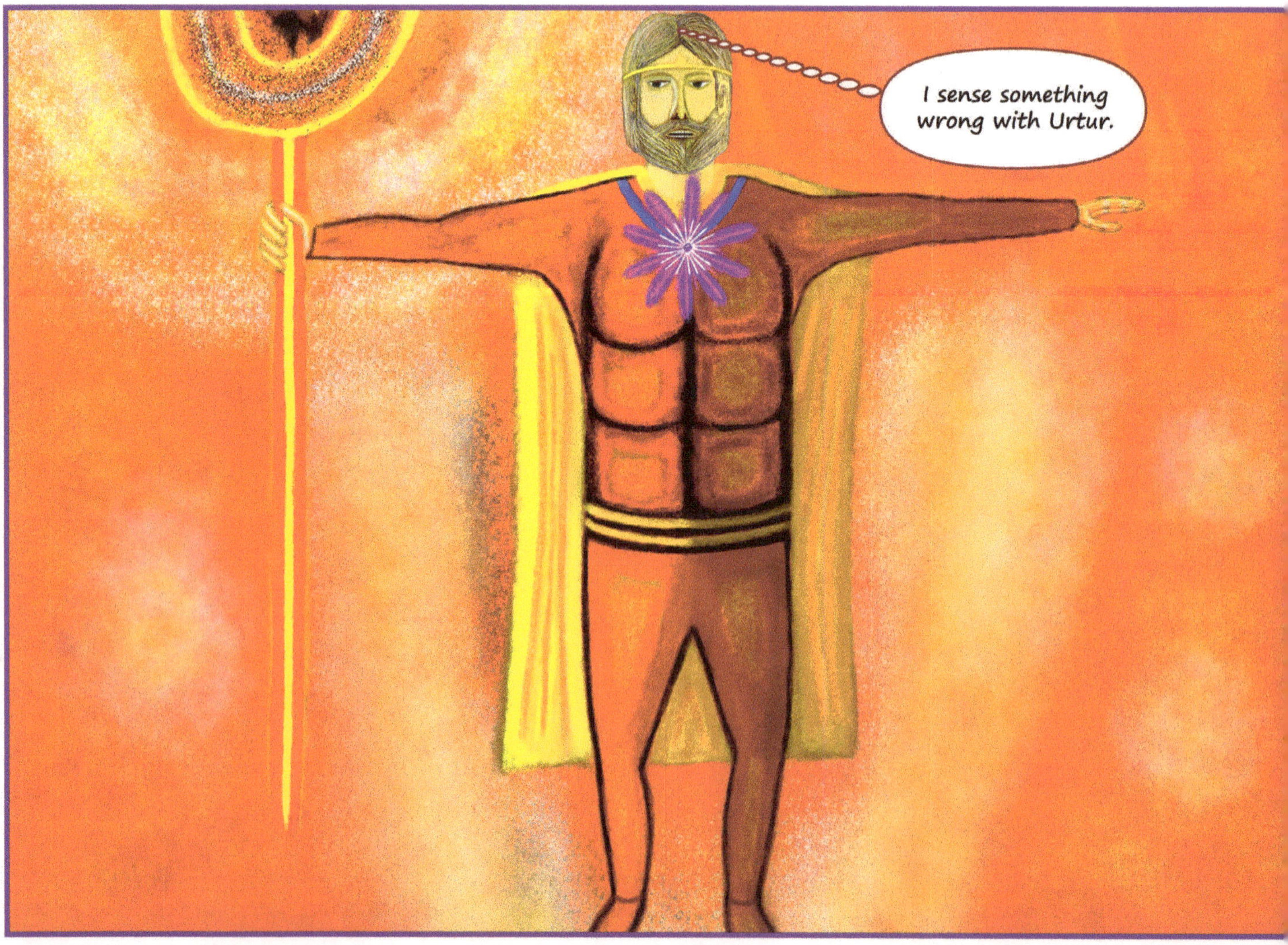

I sense something wrong with Urtur.

Anormayne, I lost sight of Falonayus. He must be using his Crown of Drakaar to make himself invisible.
Investigate the Temple of the Obelisk. I shall await you at the Mount of the Heavens near the portal.

Anormayne, you have arrived!

Falonayus transferred the soul of Protheus into Urtur, Anormayne! Now Urtur calls himself Protur.
I sensed this as I approached the temple, Ellenos.

Falonayus is taking Protur to a portal on the Mount of the Heavens. He plans to send him to a world called Urth.
How do you know this?

In his arrogance, Falonayus removed his Crown of Drakaar, allowing Gabriolus to read his thoughts.
He taunts us. We must stop him!

How can I help?
Resume your prior duties as high priestess, while I pursue Protur.

I shall do as you ask, Anormayne. What is your plan?
I shall go to the Mount of the Heavens, stop Protur from entering the portal, or follow him through the portal.

Gabriolus is on his way to the portal this very moment.
Anormayne, I hope you can succeed where I have failed!

Ellenos, your action saved the Promosatti!
Proceed to Promosthenia. Your journey will distract Falonayus, as I join Gabriolus at the portal.
Calayre can remain here as keeper of this temple, while you serve Promos as high priestess.
I will leave immediately.

Thank you for your confidence in me.
Good fortune in your travels, Anormayne.
Thank you.
Farewell, Ellenos.

Farewell, Anormayne.

Falonayus, I shall have justice!

The Promosatti are leaving for Promosthenia.

I sense Gabriolus near the Mount of the Heavens.

Chapter Five

Portal of the Heavens

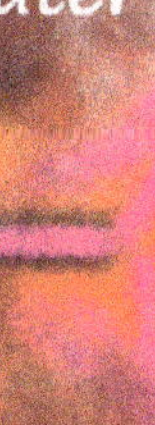

One more mountain
range to cross...

I sense Gabriolus
near the peak.

Gabriolus, I am behind you.
Anormayne, we go into battle!

Protur, I have activated the portal.
I shall attack Anormayne and Gabriolus to allow time for you to enter it!

Our defensive shields are holding!
Go now, Protur!

Protur, stop!

Falonayus, I banish you with the holy light of the Divine!

58

Gabriolus, I cannot stand your Divine light!

Anormayne, I shall pursue Falonayus. Proceed into the portal after Protur.

This void is beautiful yet terrifying!

I see Protur ahead!

I am approaching Vellorum!

I am traveling through it!

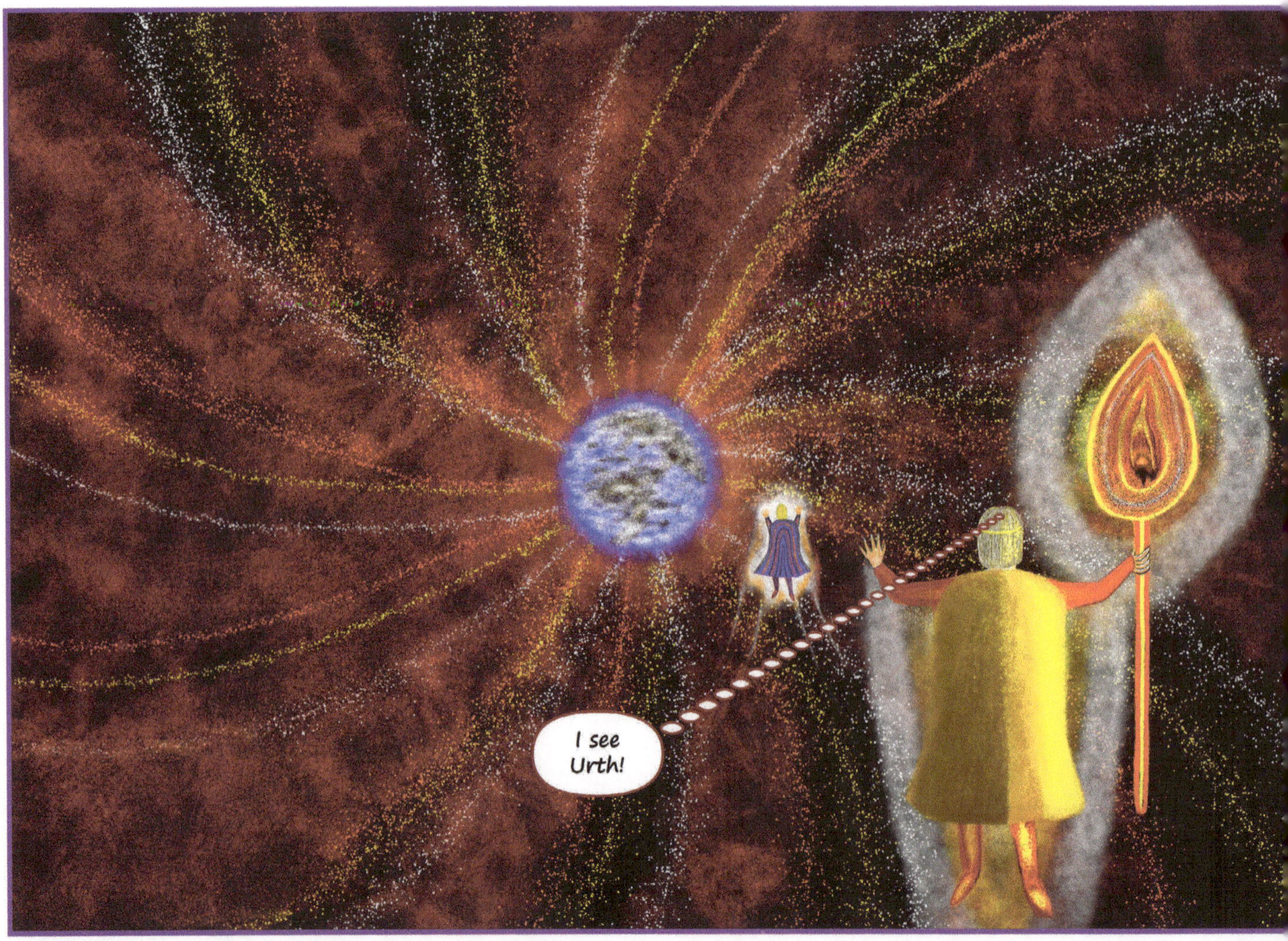

I see Urth!

We are being pulled to different locations!

Protur is traveling to another land!

Chapter Six

Protur Arrives in Spyrta
East Road
North Road
To Troyos
To Etrusus and Royma
Kingdom of Grace
South Road
Athenos
Spyrta
To Carthos
Sea of Medoya

What is this?

Lyria, I sense conflict in this man!
Penelope, a man flies down from the sky, and you worry about his thoughts?

I am your war god. Kneel before me, and I shall lead you to glory!
I obey only Thalos. You will answer to him!

Thalos, you will lead your army under my command.
I shall teach you with my Spyrtan spear!

You will do as I wish, or I shall kill you where you stand!
I cannot breath!

Behold my power!

Kneel!

Run for your life!

By kneeling, you saved your lives!
Thalos, prepare the army to move. I have an old friend to visit!
Yes, sire!

Chapter Seven

Mountains of Alpos
Anormayne Arrives in Etrusus
To Spyrta and Athenos
Etrusan Forest
Etrusus
North Road
Royma
South Road
Kingdom of Italos
To Carthos
67
Sea of Medoya

This forest is secluded. I hope to land without detection.

They have not noticed me yet.
We will keep a watchful eye Princess Imwolyn.
The forest is unusually quiet for an early morning hunt.

She is a princess, Durlyn. She has such a beautiful mind.
I never taught you about women, Anormayne, because I never understood them. Perhaps you should introduce yourself.

68

I have the undeniable feeling that I am being observed by multiple individuals.

I sense enemies ready for an ambush!
Anormayne, shall I launch a spiritual projectile to destroy these enemies?
We should exercise caution before we wield such power on this alien world!

Anormayne, use the fear ritual.

We must stop for a moment. I think I heard something.

Sar Fayle!

AAAGGGHHH!

Is this a Carthan ambush?
Who did this to you?

That man behind you cast a spell upon us!

It is my pleasure to meet you, my princess. I am Anormayne.

You are not from around here, are you Anormayne?
You are most astute, princess. How did you know?

I have hunted these lands with my father, King Ralstos, since I was a young girl.
I would know if a mage walked these lands, wielding power as you do.
Yes, princess.

You may call me Imwolyn. My father will tell you that I have never acted like a princess.
We will travel to see him now.
As you wish, Imwolyn.

Anormayne, keep a close eye on the Carthans, as we journey to Etrusus.

Chapter Eight

Visit with the King

The royal palace is ahead.

My father awaits us inside.

Father, I brought a surprise for you from my hunt.

What is your surprise, my dear daughter?

74

I bring to you a mage named Anormayne, and three Carthan prisoners.

May I retire to my chambers, father? I am fatigued after today's excitement.
Of course, Imwolyn. I will send for you later to join me, and our new guest, for dinner.
Send your mage, Anormayne, over to see me.

Anormayne, thank you for assisting my daughter today.
She seems quite capable of taking care of herself, sire.
Yes, she is quite strong. She will make a fine queen one day. Tell me more about your magic powers.
My power comes to me from the Divine, Creator of this world.

We have many gods. What makes your Divine different?
I am His high priest. I have served Him all my life. I will continue to serve Him as long as I live.
I honor Him with my actions, and He sends His angel to protect me. I obey His will above all.
This conversation interests me. We will talk more about your Divine over dinner.

Sire, Carthans kidnapped Princess Imwolyn, freed the prisoners, and escaped into the forest!

Ready the army! We march into the Etrusan forest immediately!

Let me go with you to finish what I started, sire!
Very well, Anormayne. Do not forget that my daughter's life is at stake. I hold you responsible for her safety!

Etrusans, follow me to save your princess, and protect our kingdom!

Anormayne, you are already familiar with our Etrusan forest.

Their trail leads deeper into the forest.

The Carthan fortress stands before us. We wait until dark for the rescue.
Yes, sire.

Etrusans, follow me!
Anormayne, remain concealed. When I signal, unleash your magic!

Move very quietly. We are almost inside the fortress.

It is an ambush! Fight for Etrusus and Imwolyn!

Etrusans, fight your way to the dungeon to rescue our princess!

AAAGGGHHH!
Die Ralstos!

Anormayne, help me!

Sar Lavayle!

Joffar, Sar Prayle!

79

Sire, I have to get you back to Etrusus!
I want to see my daughter!

Princess Imwolyn, please come quickly!
Father!

Anormayne, heal my father please!
Imwolyn, hold him up, and I shall do what I can!

Sar Hayle!

I have stopped your bleeding sire, but you have lost much blood!
We must take you back to Etrusus. Please rest for a moment while I speak with the Carthan prisoners.

The dungeon is ahead.

The Carthan prisoners are inside.

General Agravos is waiting to speak with you, Anormayne.

You slaughtered my soldiers without mercy!
You invaded Etrusus, kidnapped Princess Imwolyn, and gravely wounded King Ralstos!

I have no time to argue! You have one chance to save yourself and your remaining men, or suffer the same fate you just witnessed!
I need your alliance in the coming battle. I shall send for you here when I need you!

The Carthans have pledged loyalty to Etrusus. We will take the king home now.
We will leave Etrusans in this fortress, to observe our new allies and encourage their good behavior.

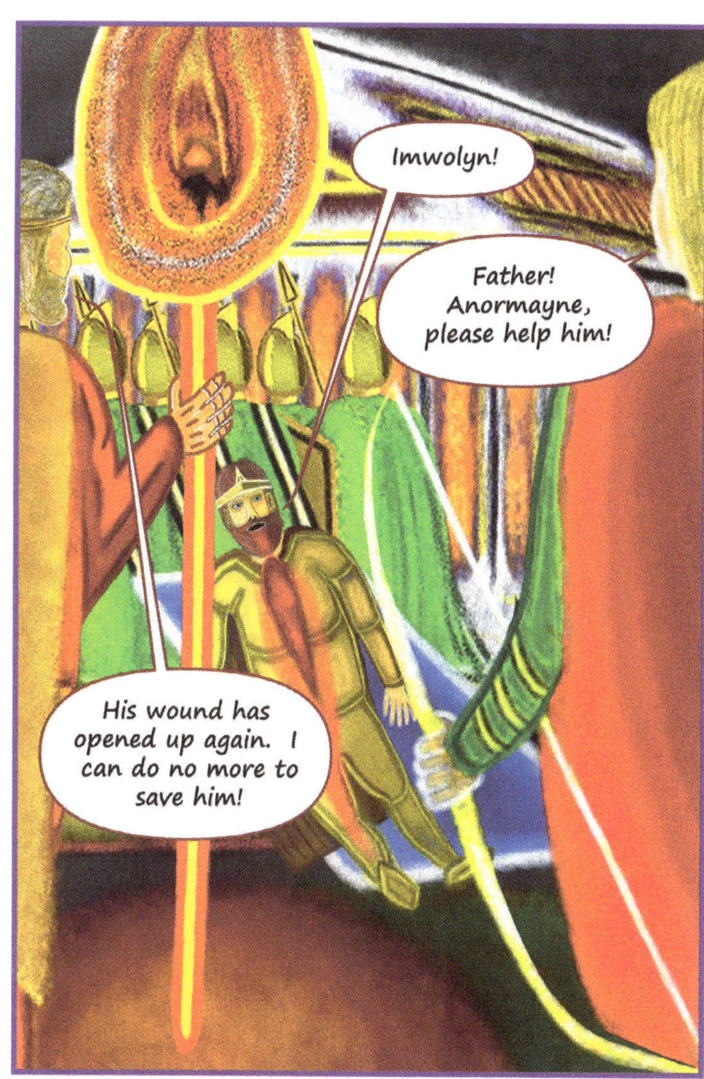

Imwolyn!
Father! Anormayne, please help him!
His wound has opened up again. I can do no more to save him!

Father, you cannot leave me. I need you!

Imwolyn, you must rule Etrusus now. It is my time to go to Anormayne's Divine. Build a funeral pyre for me!

Father, I love you!

Farewell father.

Chapter Nine

Mountains of Alpos
Protur Marches toward Etrusus
North Road
Etrusan Forest
Protur's camp
Kingdom of Grace
Etrusus
Royma
East Road
South Road
Kingdom of Italos
South Road
Spyrta
To Carthos
Sea of Medoya
85

We camp
here.

Thalos, send
scouts into those
mountains. I sense
Anormayne near.

Sire!

What is the
status of the
army, Thalos?
The Athenons joined our
Spyrtans after hearing
of your power.
Also, two priestesses
from the Temple of Apollos
wish to see you.
Very well.
Send them in.

Who are you?
I am Penelope, and she is Lyria. We are priestesses of the temple which you destroyed in Spyrta.
I have come to tell you my vision of your upcoming battle.

Continue.
I have seen your defeat, sire.
Leave now!
I sense good in you. Please turn back while you can!

What is this?

I sense weakness in you, Protur!
I shall not fail you, master!
If you falter, I shall convert Anormayne to my cause!

Thalos, prepare the army to march!

Chapter Ten

An Unexpected Ally Arrives

Anormayne, thank you for saving my life twice, and healing my father's wounds!
I wish I could have saved him! He told me to await his signal. When he called to me, he was already mortally wounded!

My mother died during my birth. My father raised me to be strong and independent.
He said a man would arrive who would care for me. I believe you are that man!
I care for you, so I must be honest. I did not travel here for you.
I came here in pursuit of my apprentice, who follows an evil path now.

Queen Imwolyn, the Roymans have arrived!

I am Tellorus Rex, King of Royma!

Imwolyn, I shall take you as my wife and queen. I have occupied Etrusus with my army to protect my new queen and kingdom!
Anormayne!

Tellorus, I challenge you to combat! May the winner dictate his terms to the defeated!
It shall be my pleasure to kill you in front of my army, my new queen, and her subjects!

Die priest!

Sar Fayle!

AAAGGGHHH!

Tellorus Rex, you will follow me north with your Royman army, to meet an invading army of Spyrtans and Athenons.

As you command, sire!

Anormayne, I shall lead my Etrusan army beside you to face this invasion!
We will combine our forces with our Carthan allies at the fortress!

Chapter Eleven

Mountains of Alpos
Battle in the Mountains
North Road
Fortress
Protur's camp
Kingdom of Grace
Etrusus
Etrusan Forest
Royma
East Road
South Road
Kingdom of Italos
South Road
Spyrta
To Carthos
Sea of Medoya

We have reached the mountains.

We camp here.

Follow me into my tent. We must make battle plans.

We must make haste with these plans. In my mind I see Protur, who is less than a one day march away!

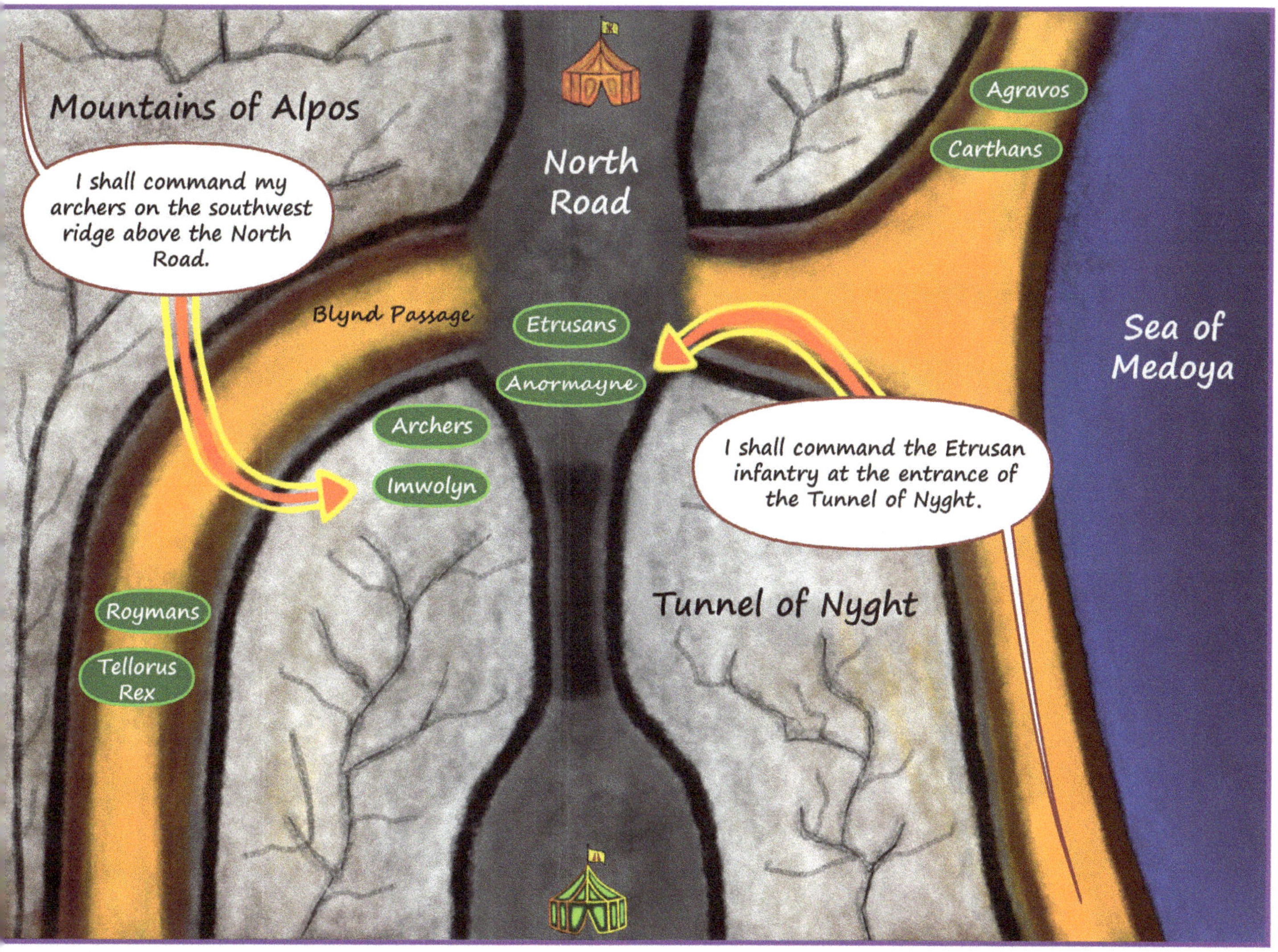

Mountains of Alpos
North Road
Agravos
Carthans
Sea of Medoya
I shall command my archers on the southwest ridge above the North Road.
Blynd Passage
Etrusans
Anormayne
Archers
Imwolyn
I shall command the Etrusan infantry at the entrance of the Tunnel of Nyght.
Roymans
Tellorus Rex
Tunnel of Nyght

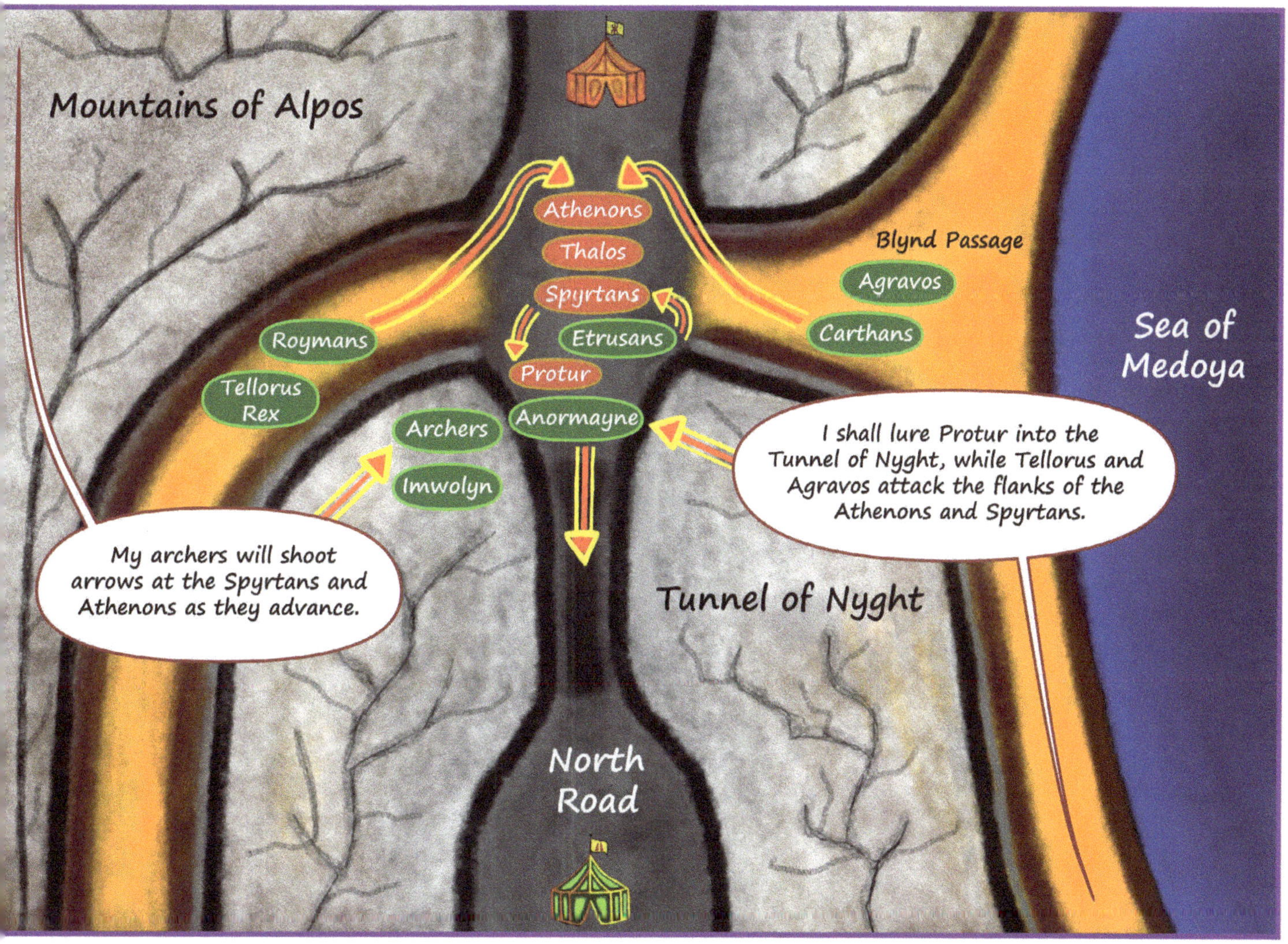

Mountains of Alpos
North Road
Athenons
Thalos
Spyrtans
Blynd Passage
Agravos
Carthans
Sea of Medoya
Roymans
Etrusans
Tellorus Rex
Protur
Archers
Anormayne
Imwolyn
I shall lure Protur into the Tunnel of Nyght, while Tellorus and Agravos attack the flanks of the Athenons and Spyrtans.
My archers will shoot arrows at the Spyrtans and Athenons as they advance.
Tunnel of Nyght
North Road

We should get a little rest before we deploy our forces.
I must investigate something outside.

Anormayne, I have a proposal for you!
Falonayus!

Follow me, and greet Protur as a brother. Together we can rule the galaxy, and avoid war!
I am a man of peace. I do not want war!

Anormayne, be strong!
Do not listen to his lies!

I cannot stand the Divine light!

Win your battle, Anormayne! I shall keep Falonayus occupied.
You and your kind must be from Mount Olympus or beyond. All I know is that I love you, Anormayne!
Imwolyn, I love you too!

I am in position.

Imwolyn is in position.

Tellorus is in position.

Agravos is in position.

At last dear friend, we meet again. Now I am your master. I shall teach your lesson.
Come to see me, Protur!

I must lure Protur into the Tunnel of Nyght.

98

Spyrtans and Athenons, attack!

Roymans, attack the western flank!
Carthans, attack the eastern flank!

I am Queen Imwolyn. Lower your weapons and surrender!

Spyrtans and Athenons, obey Queen Imwolyn immediately!

My army has lost its will to fight. I shall deal with them after I finish with you, my old friend!
Protur, this battle is over. Renounce evil. Return to the Promosatti as my brother!

Your choice of words is ironic. Anormayne, I am your brother!

No, Protheus! I do not believe you!

Falron, Dryelle, and Durlyn could not destroy me because of my identity. Join me, brother. We can rule the galaxy together!

Durlyn, Sar Shayle!

I see you have made your decision. Die, brother!
Durlyn, your spiritual shield is holding!

Joffar, Sar Prayle!

AAAGGGHHH!
Joffar, your spiritual projectile hit Protur!

Sar Sayle!
Protheus, come forth from Urtur!

Urtur, welcome back. I feared you were lost!
Thank you for saving me, master.

You have captured Protheus, Anormayne!
Falonayus has blasted through the roof!

Protheus is mine. I shall take him to Promos, to war against the Promosatti!
Anormayne, you cannot hold Protheus. Falonayus is too powerful!

Falonayus, I shall return for my brother, Protheus!

Urtur, welcome to our new world, Urth.
Thank you, Anormayne. It seems so long since we stood together on our home planet, Promos.

We have won a great victory today!
Joffar, are you ready to join Durlyn in Shor Brayle, for your journey to the Oververse?

Yes, Gabriolus, I am ready for my eternal rest.

Are you ready, Durlyn?
Yes. Proceed with the spiritual transfer ritual.

Sar Sayle!

After I take Durlyn and Joffar to the Oververse, I shall find Falonayus and Protheus! Await me on Urth until I return.

Anormayne, you are alive! I was so afraid for you, my love!
Imwolyn, allow me to introduce my apprentice, Urtur.
Protheus has left me. Only Urtur remains.

Urtur, allow me to introduce Penelope.
I knew there was good inside you!
It is my pleasure to meet you, Penelope.

Penelope told me she tried to talk you out of your invasion of Etrusus.
I do not remember anything I did under the control of Protheus.

Do not worry, Urtur. Penelope has graciously agreed to assist you in your new duties in my kingdom.
I will assist Anormayne with his new duties, as well.

Warriors of Spyrta and Athenos, go in peace to your kingdoms. Protur lives no more!

We return to Etrusus for a feast to celebrate our great victory, granted to us by Gabriolus and the Divine!
We have much to discuss!

103

GLOSSARY OF THE ANCIENTS

Main Characters	Pronunciation	Description
Anormayne	Ă nor māyne	High Priest of the Promosatti, master of Urtur, and brother of Protheus
Calayre	KĂ lär	Keeper of the Temple of the Obelisk
Dromosatti	drō mō SAH tē	Dark Promosatti who follow Falonayus
Dryelle	drē EL	High Priestess of the Promosatti, wife of Falron, and mother of Anormayne and Protheus
Durlyn	DUR lĭn	Keeper of the Crypt of Dromos, High Priest of the Promosatti, and master of Anormayne
Ellenos	ĔL en os	Keeper of the Temple of the Obelisk, and High Priestess of the Promosatti
Falonayus	fă lun ĀY us	Ruler of the Underverse
Falron	FĂL ron	High Priest of the Promosatti, husband of Dryelle, and father of Anormayne and Protheus
Gabriolus	gab rē Ó lus	Guardian angel of the Promosatti
Imwolyn	ĬM wō lin	Princess/Queen of Etrusus, and daughter of Ralstos
Joffar	Ja FAR	Apprentice of Durlyn whose spirit inhabits the staff of Durlyn and Anormayne
Promosatti	prō mō SAH tē	Followers of the Divine, Creator of the universe
Protheus	PRŌ thē us	High Promosatti priest corrupted by Falonayus, leader of the Dromosatti, and son of Falron and Dryelle
Protur	PRŌ tur	Urtur transformed through the spiritual transfer of Protheus into his body
Urtur	ŌŌR tur	Apprentice of Anormayne
Ralstos	RĂL stōs	King of Etrusus, and father of Imwolyn

Rituals	Translation	Description
Sar Fayle	Spiritual Activation Ritual Fear	Creates fear in affected individuals allowing mind control
Sar Hayle	Spiritual Activation Ritual Heal	Heals individuals who have mild to moderate wounds
Sar Lavayle	Spiritual Activation Ritual Levitate	Levitates individuals in an up, down, or horizontal direction
Sar Prayle	Spiritual Activation Ritual Projectile	Launches a spiritual projectile at one or more individuals
Sar Sayle	Spiritual Activation Ritual Sustain	Sustains spiritual energy for transfer to a body or object
Sar Shayle	Spiritual Activation Ritual Shield	Creates a spiritual shield for one or more individuals

Locations	Description
Athenos	Urth citadel of the Kingdom of Grace
Carthos	Urth citadel south of the Kingdom of Italos and the Sea of Medoya, ruled by Agravos
Crypt of Dromos	Underground labyrinth housing Durlyn, Protheus, and the Dromosatti imprisoned from the War of Dromos
Dungeon	Prison inside the Crypt of Dromos housing Protheus
Etrusus	Urth citadel of the Kingdom of Italos
Gate of Drakaar	Entrance to the Underverse
Kingdom of Grace	Home of the Urth citadels Athenos and Spyrta
Kingdom of Italos	Home of the Urth citadels Etrusus and Royma
Mountains of Alpos	Mountain range north of Etrusus
Mountains of Fyre	Volcanic mountain range surrounding Promosthenia
Mount of the Heavens	Entrance to the Oververse, and site of the Portal of the Heavens
Oververse	Home of the Divine and Gabriolus
Pillars of Dromos	Memorial built on top of the Crypt of Dromos to honor the Promosatti victory in the War of Dromos
Plane of Despayre	Desert wasteland leading to the Gate of Drakaar, and site of the War of Dromos
Portal of the Heavens	Built by Gabriolus to transport mortals throughout the universe
Promos	Home world of the Promosatti and the Dromosatti
Promosthenia	Home of the Temple of Towers
Royma	Urth citadel of the Kingdom of Italos, ruled by Tellorus Rex
Spyrta	Urth citadel of the Kingdom of Grace, ruled by Thalos, and home of Penelope
Sea of Medoya	Urth sea bordering the Kingdoms of Italos and Grace
Temple of the Obelisk	Home of Ellenos, built by Durlyn to honor the Promosatti victory in the War of Dromos
Temple of Towers	Home of Anormayne, and High Temple of the Promosatti
Tunnel of Nyght	Passage through the Mountains of Alpos, and site of the final battle between Anormayne and Protur
Underverse	Home of Falonayus
Urth	Home world of Athenos, Carthos, Etrusus, Royma, and Spyrta
Vellorum	Collapsing dwarf star near Promos, used by Gabriolus to create a wormhole, the Portal of the Heavens
Vulcanum	Giant star near Promos

Lore	Description
Amulet of Shorcuyle	Amulet of good wielded by Ellenos to dispel Falonayus and Protur from the Temple of the Obelisk
Joffar	Staff of Durlyn and Anormayne which houses the spirit of Joffar until he ascends to the Oververse
Shor Brayle	Soul Bringer of the Heavens used by Gabriolus to transport the spirits of Durlyn and Joffar to the Oververse
Shor Tayle	Soul Teacher of the Heavens, and Prophet of the Divine, sent to Urth to spread His message

Dedicated
to Margaret
and Constance,
for editing
and many
creative
contributions
to this
graphic
novel.

Continue the epic journey of Anormayne and Imwolyn with Quest of the Ancients: Book Two of the Ancients Saga, available 2021!